Disney PRINCESS

Mulan's Perfect Present

By Cynthea Liu

Illustrated by Alan Batson and the Disney Storybook Art Team

A Random House PICTUREBACK® Book

Random House 🏠 New York

Copyright © 2018 Disney Enterprises, Inc. All rights reserved. Published in the United States by Random House Children's Books, a division of Penguin Random House LLC, 1745 Broadway, New York, NY 10019, and in Canada by Penguin Random House Canada Limited, Toronto, in conjunction with Disney Enterprises, Inc. Pictureback, Random House, and the Random House colophon are registered trademarks of Penguin Random House LLC.
rhcbooks.com
ISBN 978-0-7364-3753-0
Printed in the United States of America
10 9 8 7 6 5 4 3 2 1

Mulan was nervous. Tomorrow was the tournament of the Imperial Courts—and it was her father's birthday. She wanted to win him the prized scroll. It would be the perfect birthday present!

"Do you think I'll win?" Mulan asked her father.

"A better question is will you honor our family by doing your best?" he replied.

The next morning, Mulan practiced with her friends Mushu, Cri-Kee, and Little Brother.

"Can we fight with you?" asked Mushu, the little dragon.

"Thanks, Mushu," said Mulan. "But I have to do this on my own."

"Good luck!" said the dragon.

Later, in the Great Circle, the crowd cheered while the contestants prepared to start.

Mulan saw her family in the stands and remembered her father's advice. She would do her very best.

The master of ceremonies
introduced the contestants and
explained the rules. Each warrior
would battle one opponent at a
time in the Great Circle. The winner
would advance to the next round.

When Mushu heard
Mulan's name, he cheered.

The first round was archery.
Mulan's opponent was big
and skilled.

But Mulan hit the targets faster.

She won!

Mulan had to battle with a staff in the next round.
Mushu was cheering so much, he almost fell into the
Great Circle! That distracted Mulan, but only for a moment.

She quickly recovered and split her opponent's
weapon in two. She won again!

Mulan defeated opponent
after opponent. The scroll was
almost hers!

Soon there were only two warriors left: Mulan and
Wan Na Pu.
Wan Na Pu was the fiercest competitor of all!

For the final round, the warriors were able to choose their weapons. Wan picked up two tridents. Mulan selected the imperial sword of China.

Wan was a strong and skilled fighter. But Mulan soon gained the advantage.

Mulan's friends formed a tower and cheered from the sidelines as Mulan outfought Wan.

The prized scroll was almost hers, when . . .

. . . Mushu lost his balance! All three friends fell
into the ring, right in the path of Wan's trident.

Mulan had to save them! She turned away from her opponent and chopped down a nearby beam, hoping it would block the trident.

Mulan's plan worked! But it also caused her to step outside the Great Circle.

"Disqualified!" called the master of ceremonies.

"I'm sorry," Mulan told her father afterward. "I lost the tournament and the scroll I promised you. Your birthday is ruined."

"Mulan, I do not need you to win me a scroll," said her father. "You bravely saved your friends today and proved to be a true warrior. That was the perfect present."

The next day, Jasmine and Abu had a yummy feast at the palace with lots of new friends!

That gave Jasmine and Abu an idea. When they got home that evening, they went straight to the palace kitchen and spoke to the cook.

Abu knew his young friends needed the food more than he did.

Jasmine wanted to share with them, too!

And he was. Jasmine found her friend
sitting with some children from the city.
He was sharing his food with them.

She found another banana peel on the building's ledge, but no Abu.

She vaulted to the next building and found some bread crumbs. Abu had to be close!

Jasmine saw something on top of another building. She vaulted to the rooftop.

"A banana peel!" she exclaimed.

Jasmine and the Magic Carpet flew up to the nearest rooftop.

"Abu!" Jasmine called. "Where are you?"

Jasmine gave the cap to the Magic Carpet and
looked around. Had the cap fallen from one of
the nearby buildings?

Jasmine spotted Abu's cap on the street below.
"He never goes anywhere without that!" she said.

"Let's look for more clues!" said Jasmine.
She hopped onto the Magic Carpet, and they
set out over the kingdom.

Jasmine was worried. She asked
the Magic Carpet for help searching
the palace grounds, and he soon
found an apple core.

. . . except the cook.

"He stopped by earlier and took a loaf of bread, some apples, and a bunch of bananas," she told Jasmine. "Then he left the palace."

Jasmine searched the palace for Abu.
She asked everyone if they had seen him,
but nobody had . . .

One evening, Abu didn't show up for dinner. He never missed a meal!

"Where is he?" Jasmine wondered aloud.

Jasmine especially loved sharing delicious meals
with her family and friends.

And Abu liked to play big tricks on Jasmine.

Jasmine liked to play
little tricks on Abu.

Princess Jasmine had always been best friends with Rajah. Now she was friends with Abu, too!

Jasmine's New Friends

By Victoria Saxon

Illustrated by Alan Batson and the Disney Storybook Art Team

A Random House PICTUREBACK® Book

Random House New York

Copyright © 2018 Disney Enterprises, Inc. All rights reserved. Published in the United States by Random House Children's Books, a division of Penguin Random House LLC, 1745 Broadway, New York, NY 10019, and in Canada by Penguin Random House Canada Limited, Toronto, in conjunction with Disney Enterprises, Inc. Pictureback, Random House, and the Random House colophon are registered trademarks of Penguin Random House LLC.
rhcbooks.com
ISBN 978-0-7364-3753-0
Printed in the United States of America
10 9 8 7 6 5 4 3 2 1